ZIGGY

Baxter
Bear
Buddy
Chewy and Chica
Cody
Flash
Goldie
Honey
Jack
Lucky
Maggie and Max
Muttley
Noodle
Patches
Princess
Pugsley
Rascal
Scout
Shadow
Snowball
Sweetie
Ziggy

THE PUPPY PLACE

ZIGGY

ELLEN MILES

SCHOLASTIC INC.

New York   Toronto   London   Auckland
Sydney   Mexico City   New Delhi   Hong Kong

For Joe, Anne, and Sofie

ISBN 978-0-545-25395-6

Cover art by Tim O'Brien
Original cover design by Steve Scott

12 11 10 9 8 7 6   11 12 13 14 15/0

Printed in the U.S.A.   40

First printing, November 2010

CHAPTER ONE

"Take your dogs on around, please."

Charles Peterson cheered and clapped along with the rest of the crowd as he watched nine of the prettiest golden retrievers he had ever seen prance around in a circle. They held their heads and tails high, and their silky coats rippled and shone in the sun. After the dog show judge told the handlers to trot their dogs around the ring, she took some time to look over the retrievers more closely, checking their teeth and stroking their coats.

Charles tried to decide which one he liked best. Some really were golden—but others were paler or reddish or copper-colored like a bright, shiny new penny. They all had feathery tails, silky-looking ears, proud heads, and bright eyes set in happy, eager faces.

"Wow." Charles decided that he couldn't decide. "They're all so beautiful."

"Aren't they?" His aunt Amanda smiled down at him. "This dog show is my favorite event of the fall, every year."

"It's my new favorite, too," said Charles's older sister, Lizzie, who stood on the other side of their aunt. "Thanks for bringing us, Aunt Amanda. This is better than Halloween."

Charles thought for a moment. *Better than Halloween? Hmmm. Chocolate or dogs. Chocolate or dogs.* Which did he like better? He sure did love chocolate, but still, it was really no contest. "You're right," he told his sister. "This might even beat Halloween—for a dog lover."

There was no question that Charles, his aunt, and his sister were all dog lovers. Aunt Amanda even made her living working with dogs: She ran a doggy day-care center called Bowser's Backyard, where people could leave their dogs for the day while they were at work. And Charles and Lizzie, along with their parents and their younger brother the Bean, whose real name was Adam—not that anybody ever called him that—were a foster family for puppies. That meant that when they met a puppy who needed a home, they kept it and took care of it until they could find it the perfect forever family.

The Petersons had fostered lots of puppies, and Charles had loved every single one of them. It wasn't always easy to give them up when the time came. Luckily, the best one of all had come to stay. Buddy, the cutest puppy ever, had started out as a foster puppy, but the Petersons had decided to keep him. Now Buddy was a member of the family.

But as cute as Buddy was, with his soft brown fur and the white spot in the shape of a heart on his chest, he had not been allowed to come along to the dog show. Neither had Aunt Amanda's four dogs—three pugs and Bowser, the golden retriever her business was named after. Aunt Amanda had said that there would be way too many dogs, and way too much distraction, for it to be easy or fun to have their own dogs with them. She had been right, too. Charles could see that now. Anyway, it turned out that he did not miss Buddy at all. He didn't have *time* to miss him. Charles was too busy taking in all the sights and sounds of the dog show.

It was so cool how the judge told the handlers what to do. Following her orders, they walked their dogs around the ring or trotted them up and back so that the judge could watch the way the dogs ran. Sometimes the judge had the handlers make the dogs pose like statues while she took another close look at their teeth and tails and everything in between.

"To win in a dog show," Aunt Amanda had explained, "a dog has to be the best example of its breed. There is a certain way each breed is supposed to look, called a standard. That's what the judges will look for—how well each dog meets the standard."

"I know Buddy can't be in the show, because it's only for purebreds and he's a mixed-breed dog. But what about Bowser?" Charles asked. "He's just as good-looking as the rest of these golden retrievers. How come you don't enter him in a show?"

"Bowser is a handsome guy," Aunt Amanda agreed. "But he does not meet the breed standard. He's a little too big, and his chest isn't exactly the way it should be. But he's my best boy and I could never love anybody more."

A man next to Aunt Amanda smiled. "That's how we all feel about our dogs, isn't it? They don't have to be champions in the ring to be champions in our hearts."

"Couldn't have said it better myself, Nathan," said Aunt Amanda. "I know you feel that way about Sally."

Aunt Amanda seemed to know every person at this dog show—and most of the dogs, as well.

Lizzie didn't know any of the people or their dogs' names, but she knew every breed. "There's a Plott hound!" she'd say. "Check out that schipperke!"

Charles barely knew a Plott hound from a Pomeranian, but he didn't care. He loved every dog he saw, and that day he was seeing hundreds of them. He loved their silky coats; their happy, smiling faces with their tongues lolling out; their perky ears and wagging tails. He loved the doggy smells everywhere and the sounds of panting and barking. He wished he could hug every single dog at that show.

In the ring, the judge finally made her decisions. She handed a big blue ribbon to the handler of the shiniest, goldest retriever in the group. The handler burst into happy tears and threw her arms around the judge, then knelt to hug the dog.

Charles didn't know why, but it almost made him feel like crying, too.

"Later today, that golden retriever will represent his breed in the best of group competition," explained Aunt Amanda. "Golden retrievers belong to the sporting group, along with labs and other athletic dogs. Pugs are in the toy group, and dogs like border collies are in the herding group. Each group will have its own competition, and then the winners of those will be in the very last competition, for best in show. You won't believe how exciting that is."

They started to walk around the grounds again.

"Look! A wiener dog." Charles pointed to an adorable short-legged puppy with a long, sausage-shaped body.

"You mean a *dachshund*," Lizzie said. "That is a short-haired dachshund, to be exact."

"Whatever. Look at him. He's so cute." He really was just about the cutest dog Charles had ever seen—next to Buddy, of course. He was black and tan, with a silky-smooth shiny coat, huge hot-chocolate eyes, a long pointy nose, and big floppy ears. The puppy looked right back at Charles and pulled on his leash, his little tail wagging so hard and fast that it was nothing but a blur.

The announcer said something, but Charles wasn't paying attention. All he could do was stare at that dog. He was dying to pet him—or better yet, pick him up and hug him—but he knew he couldn't do that without asking the owner first.

"Aunt Amanda," Lizzie said, "the announcer just said that pugs are in Ring Two right now."

"Can't miss that," said Aunt Amanda. She pulled at Charles's sleeve as she started off in the opposite direction. "Let's go, Charles."

"You go," said Charles. "I'll catch up." And he took off at a trot to get a closer look at the wiener dog.

CHAPTER TWO

"Your dog is really cute. Can I pet him?" Charles asked the woman holding the dachshund's leash. She was as big and round as the puppy was tiny and long. "My name's Charles Peterson. My family fosters puppies, so I'm used to dogs."

She smiled at him. "Hi, Charles. I'm Rosie," she said. "And thanks for asking first. You're welcome to pet him. Ziggy loves kids."

"Ziggy?" Charles asked. "What a great name." He knelt down to pat the dog. "Hi, Ziggy."

Ziggy put his paws up on Charles's knee. His tail wagged even faster. Charles patted the puppy's head. His short hair was soft and smooth and warm under Charles's hand. The puppy looked up at Charles with those huge trusting eyes and snuffled at Charles's fingers.

Hi! Do I smell bacon? Yum!

Charles giggled. "I think he smells my breakfast on my hands," he told Rosie. He laughed again as Ziggy tried to climb into his lap. "Is Ziggy in the dog show?"

Rosie shook her head. "Not this boy," she said. "My husband and I breed dachshunds, and we have four other dogs in the show today. But Ziggy—well, Ziggy's not what we call show quality."

"What do you mean?" Charles asked. "He seems perfect to me."

"It's his overbite." Rosie shook her head. "See the way he looks a little bucktoothed, with his top teeth forward? That's what is known as a major fault, and it means he will never win a blue ribbon in the ring. We won't breed him, either, since we don't want more puppies with that problem."

"Wow." Charles thought Ziggy's face was adorable, overbite or not. What was the big deal? "That's too bad."

Rosie shrugged. "We have plenty of other show dogs. The sad part is that I have to find a home for him. I'm pretty crazy about the little guy, but I just can't keep him. When my husband, Peter, and I got married, he promised that I could have four dogs. I bumped him up to five, then seven, then nine. But Peter drew the line at ten. I keep telling him Ziggy is a real special boy, but even I can't deny that we've already got dachshunds coming out of our ears at home, what with the moms and the dads and sometimes two litters of puppies at one time."

Charles smiled, picturing Rosie with wiener dogs coming out of her ears. He could just imagine what her house must look like, with all those dogs. "I bet lots of people would want Ziggy," he said.

"Maybe," said Rosie. "But Ziggy is seven months old, and I haven't found the right owner yet. I am very fussy about the homes my dogs go to. Dachshunds are terrific dogs, but they are not for everyone. I interview the people who want my dogs, and if they don't seem like the right owners, I won't sell them a dog."

"That's just like us," Charles said. "When my family fosters puppies, we make sure that we find each one the perfect forever family. Every dog deserves a great home."

Rosie nodded and smiled. "I agree with you one hundred percent," she said.

Charles petted Ziggy once more, wishing he could pick him up and hug him forever. Ziggy really was a special guy. But Aunt Amanda might be wondering where he was. Maybe he should head over to Ring Two and find her and Lizzie.

The loudspeaker crackled and popped, and the announcer said, "Dachshunds to Ring Five. Dachshunds to Ring Five. Judging begins in five minutes."

Rosie's hand flew to her mouth. "Oh, dear! I lost track of time. And of my husband. Where did Peter go? I have to go show one of our other dogs, and he promised to stay with Ziggy while I'm in the ring." She glanced around wildly.

Charles looked at Ziggy. Ziggy looked back at him, wrinkling his brow in a funny way. Charles almost thought he saw Ziggy wink at him.

How about it? You and me, pal.

"I could watch him," Charles said.

Rosie hesitated.

"I really do know about dogs," said Charles. "I have lots of experience. And so does my aunt. She's right around here somewhere." He waved an arm.

Rosie checked her watch. "I don't have a second to spare." She bit her lip. "Okay, Charles Peterson. Maybe I'm crazy, but I have a good feeling about you. I'm going to trust you with my Zigaroo." She handed the leash to Charles. "Hang on tight," she warned. "Ziggy loves to run. And he's a bit of a Houdini."

"A bit of a what?" Charles asked, but Rosie was already ten steps away. Charles looked down at Ziggy and tightened his grip on the leash. "Well, whatever you are, you're stuck with me. Come on, let's go find Aunt Amanda."

At Ring Two, the judge was just awarding the blue ribbon to a cute fawn-colored pug with a squashed black nose. Lizzie and Aunt Amanda clapped like crazy, along with the rest of the audience. The pug twirled around at the end of his leash, clearly loving all the attention.

"Hi," said Charles.

Aunt Amanda turned. "Charles, where have

you—" She stopped and stared down at the dachshund puppy. "Well, well, well. If it isn't Ziggy." She and Lizzie both squatted down to pat Ziggy.

"You know this puppy?" Charles asked. Of course. Aunt Amanda knew every dog for miles around. Why should he be surprised?

"Sure," said Aunt Amanda. "He's a love. Rosie's been trying forever to find a new home for him, but nobody's good enough for her Ziggy. Rosie is an excellent, responsible breeder and she really cares about where her dogs end up. But in this case, I think maybe she's just a little too attached to the pup."

"She let me hold him because she had to go show her other dachshunds," Charles explained. "I promised to take good care of him."

Aunt Amanda nodded. "I'm impressed. She must have really liked you. Rosie wouldn't let just anyone take care of the Zigster."

Charles was starting to get an idea. "I wonder...," he said.

Aunt Amanda looked at him and raised her eyebrows.

"I wonder if she'd let us foster him," he finished.

CHAPTER THREE

"Okay, we went over the bridge. Now we're in West Springfield. Take a left at the second traffic light." Charles peered at the paper in his lap. It was the day after the dog show, and he and Aunt Amanda were on their way to Rosie's house. Aunt Amanda was driving, and Charles was the navigator. That meant he had to read the directions out loud and make sure Aunt Amanda followed them correctly. They had been driving for a half hour already; Rosie lived a few towns away.

"You sure do know how to get the job done," Charles said to Aunt Amanda as they waited to make their turn. He had to hand it to his aunt. If you gave her a good idea, she could make it happen. And that was exactly what she had done with his idea about his family fostering Ziggy. She had talked to Rosie. She had talked to Mom and Dad. And now they were on their way to pick the little dachshund up and take him home. As of that day, the Petersons would have a new foster puppy—one of the cutest ones ever, in Charles's opinion.

Charles was so excited he had hardly slept at all the night before. Lizzie was excited, too, but she never got *that* excited about small dogs. She was more of a big-dog person. She had promised to help out at the animal shelter that day, so Charles and Aunt Amanda were on their own.

"Now take a right and go past the church and up the hill to the flashing yellow light," said Charles. "We'll take a left there."

"Get ready for a *lot* of dachshunds," Aunt Amanda told him. "Rosie said they would bark like crazy when we first arrive, but she promised they would settle down quickly."

One right turn and one left turn later, they pulled up to a red house with a dachshund-shaped mailbox.

"This must be the place," said Charles. He checked the number on the house, just to be sure. "Yup. Number 21. This is it." He could already hear the barking as they got out of Aunt Amanda's van and walked up the front steps.

Rosie opened the door a crack. "Come on in," she said. "Don't let anybody out."

A swarm of barking dachshunds scrabbled and slid their way toward Charles and his aunt. They all had sharp little noses, big dark soulful eyes, short legs, and wagging tails. But they were all different sizes and colors: from black and tan to solid black, from dark brown to coppery gold. And while some were short-haired, like Ziggy, others had long, feathery hair that drooped from their ears, tails, and bellies. They yipped and yapped loudly as they jumped up to greet Charles and Aunt Amanda. "Wow!" Aunt Amanda had to yell to be heard over the racket. "How many are there?"

Rosie laughed as she scooped Ziggy up into her arms and nuzzled him with her cheek. "Eleven right now. Not counting the puppies, that is, since we'll sell them when they're old enough. Some people think we're crazy. I tell them we are. We're crazy about dachshunds."

Charles sat down right there—on a doormat with a picture of a dachshund on it—and let five of the sausage dogs squirm their way onto his lap. Four others continued to jump and twirl. They leapt up onto Aunt Amanda's knees. It took a while, but finally the dogs began to settle down.

"They're great," said Charles when it was quiet enough to talk. He had never spent much time around a dachshund before. He was dying to hold Ziggy, but Rosie didn't look as if she wanted to let go of him quite yet. "I love their eyes. They all look so smart."

"Don't they?" agreed Rosie. "I always say you can see all sorts of emotions in a dachshund's eyes. Love, worry, happiness—it's all there. They're very sensitive dogs. Sometimes they even get sulky when their feelings are hurt, and you can see *that* in their eyes."

"What are their names?" Charles asked.

"Let's see. Starting with the oldest, that's my grandma dog, Candy, over there." Rosie waved at a white-faced dog off by herself on a bed in the corner. "Then we have Mikey, Penny, Schotzie, Bear, Sparky—she's the spotted one—Sis, Hans— he's kind of a bully—Pupper, Chocolate, and of course, Ziggy."

She kissed Ziggy's head. "I understand you have a younger brother," she said to Charles. "I don't usually let my dogs go to households with young children. Dachshunds aren't laid-back like golden retrievers. They won't put up with having their ears pulled or their eyes poked. But Ziggy grew up around my grandnephew, so he's used to kids."

"The Bean is used to dogs, too," Charles said. The fat brown dachshund named Hans climbed into Charles's lap and growled at the other dogs until they fled. "My brother knows he can't pull puppies' tails or kiss their noses or bother them when they're eating."

"Very good," said Rosie. "And you have a fenced yard?"

Charles nodded. He told Rosie all about his family's house and yard, and listened as she told him all about Ziggy. Ziggy wasn't exactly spoiled, the way Princess, a Yorkie the Petersons had once fostered, had been, but Rosie did seem to have a lot to say about his likes and dislikes. "Be sure to keep an eye on him," she finished. "Remember what I said about him being a Houdini."

Aunt Amanda had explained to Charles that

Harry Houdini had been a famous magician who could escape from anywhere, no matter how people tried to lock or tie him up. Now Charles nodded.

"Ziggy is a curious guy," Rosie warned. "And a dachshund who likes to follow his nose is a dachshund who could end up just about anywhere. Isn't that right, Ziggy Zigman?" She held the puppy up so she could look him in the eyes.

Ziggy licked Rosie's nose and wagged his tail.

You got it, lady!

Charles couldn't help smiling at Ziggy's cute expression. When would he finally get to hold him?

"Oh, and I almost forgot. Ziggy-wiggy doesn't like loud noises." Rosie continued with her directions. "And he prefers to eat breakfast all by himself, without any other dogs around."

"Rosie," Aunt Amanda finally said, "You couldn't ask for a better foster family than the Petersons. They will take great care of Ziggy and they will find him a terrific home."

Rosie nodded. "I know. And I really am ready to send Ziggy home with Charles. But would you like to meet our newest pups before you go?"

Still carrying Ziggy, she led them through a living room with needlepoint dachshunds on the walls, china dachshunds on the mantel, and stuffed dachshunds on the couches, then down a hall and into a big bathroom. "We use this for the whelping room, where our mom dogs have their puppies," she said. "It's a nice quiet place, away from the craziness of the rest of the house. The moms can take care of their newborn puppies in peace. And since it's a bathroom, we're in and out of here all the time. That means the puppies get used to being around people."

"Socialization," said Charles. "I know about that." He knelt down to look into a box where four tiny puppies lay squirming in a pile, mewing like little kittens. Their eyes were barely open, and their noses were flat, not pointy like the older dogs' noses.

"They're only two weeks old, a little too young to handle," said Rosie. "But if you come back in a couple of weeks, you can play with them all you want."

The puppies were cute, but Charles thought Ziggy was way cuter and much more interesting. He could hardly wait to take him home, introduce him to Buddy and the rest of the family, and play with him. He looked up at Aunt Amanda, and she must have seen the impatience in his eyes.

"I think it's time we left." She put a hand on Rosie's shoulder.

Again, she got the job done. Five minutes later, Charles and his aunt zoomed back down the road with Ziggy safely penned in the crate in the back of Aunt Amanda's van.

CHAPTER FOUR

When they arrived at home, Charles made sure that Ziggy's leash was securely clipped to his collar before he opened the crate. Then he lifted Ziggy out of the van, gave him a quick hug, and set him on the front walk. "This is your temporary home, Ziggy," he said. "What do you think?"

Ziggy ran from side to side as far as his leash would allow, sniffing everything in sight.

"I see why Rosie named you Ziggy." Charles laughed as he ran to keep up. "You like to zig and zag and zoom all over the place, don't you?"

"She was right about his curiosity, too," said Aunt Amanda. "Look at him. He's finding out everything he can about this new place."

27

Ziggy screeched to a halt and sniffed at a rose-bush. His ears perked up and his tail stood straight out.

Another dog lives here. He peed on this bush this morning.

"I bet he smells Buddy," said Charles. "That's good. Now he won't be surprised to find out that there's another dog in the house."

Ziggy zoomed over to sniff at a red-and-white mitten the Bean had dropped on the front walk. His tail began to wag.

A little person! I like little people.

Aunt Amanda scooped up the mitten. "I guess he won't be too surprised by the Bean, either," she said.

Mom and the Bean were waiting inside.

"Doggy!" cried the Bean the second Charles and Ziggy walked in.

Charles thought it was kind of amazing how little kids always knew that a dog was a dog. Tiny pointy-nosed Ziggy did not look one bit like Maggie, the huge drooly Saint Bernard puppy the Petersons had once fostered. But the Bean had known right away that they were both doggies.

"No touching," Mom reminded the Bean. "Stand very still and let the doggy sniff you." She stood right behind the Bean, her hands on his shoulders, while Charles let Ziggy go closer. Ziggy snuffled and sniffed at the Bean.

Yup, you're one of the good ones. Nice and quiet. Not the kind who will bug me or tease me.

Then the puppy licked the Bean's hand.

"Mommy," the Bean said, giggling, "The 'uppy kissed me!"

"That's good," said Mom. "He likes you." Then she knelt down to say hello to Ziggy. "I put Buddy out in the backyard," she told Charles. "I figured Ziggy should meet us one by one. Dad and Lizzie won't be home for a couple of hours." She petted Ziggy's head. "Hi, cutie," she said. "Look at those soulful eyes."

It took no time at all for Ziggy to get used to the Bean and Mom, the house, and even Buddy. After Aunt Amanda left, Charles took Ziggy outside to introduce the two puppies. They got along right away. They sniffed at each other for a few seconds, then took off on a mad chase around the yard. Charles noticed that Ziggy checked out every inch of the fence as he zoomed by. They made three complete circles before they stopped to sniff each other again. Charles was surprised at how fast Ziggy could run when he didn't have his leash on. He made Buddy look like a plodding elephant.

Mom came out on the back deck to watch. "Look at him go," she said.

"Do you think it's okay if I invite David and Sammy over to meet him?" Charles asked. "I think he's getting used to everything here okay." He couldn't wait until his two best friends saw Ziggy. They were going to love the new foster puppy.

"Sure," said Mom. "I'll bring you the phone so you can call them from out here, while you watch Ziggy. Now that I see how much energy that pup has, I think playing outside is a great idea. It won't be easy to tire this little guy out."

Sammy got there first, since he lived right next door. He rode his bike over. He and Charles and David had practically been living on their bikes lately. David rode up a few minutes later. They both loved Ziggy right away, even though he kept squirming out of their arms when they tried to hold him. All that puppy wanted to do was run, run, run.

Sammy, as usual, came up with an idea. "Maybe

we can tire him out better if we ride our bikes around," he said. "Ziggy's so fast that running with Buddy barely makes him pant."

Charles and David looked at each other. Sammy's ideas were always exciting. And maybe a little risky, too. But really, what could go wrong? The three boys buckled on their helmets and began to ride in circles around the edges of the yard, right along the Petersons' side of the fence. Buddy couldn't quite keep up as they peeled out around the corners and took off flying down the straightaways, but Ziggy *loved* the game. He barked and yipped as he galloped along after them. His short legs churned through the grass so fast that they were nothing but a blur.

Charles, David, and Sammy laughed and yelled. What a great game. Then Mom came out onto the deck. "Boys," she called. *"Boys!* Do you really think it's a good idea to teach that dog to chase someone on a bike? Charles, you know your aunt

Amanda always says that dogs who run after bikes or cars often get hurt. Anyway, I think this game is just a little too wild for Ziggy's first day."

Charles got off his bike. He knew that what Mom said was true. And he had promised Rosie that he would take good care of Ziggy. "Come on, guys," he told his friends. "Let's take Ziggy inside for a while." He looked around. "Ziggy?"

In the far corner of the yard, Buddy began to bark. Charles recognized that bark. It was Buddy's "I-see-a-squirrel" bark. He would sit and bark all day at the squirrels who climbed on the big old oak tree in the Galluccis' backyard, across the fence.

Ziggy wasn't barking. But when the boys ran over to the corner of the yard, Charles saw why. Ziggy wasn't sitting, either. Ziggy was very busy digging a tunnel underneath the fence. He was already halfway through, and all Charles could see were Ziggy's rear end, his back paws, and a crazily wagging tail as Ziggy's wild digging sent showers of dirt flying through the air.

"Hey," said Charles. "Hold on there, Houdini!" He ran to grab the puppy, but just then, one of the squirrels chattered loudly down at Ziggy. With a sharp bark, Ziggy squirted right through the tunnel he'd dug.

CHAPTER FIVE

On the other side of the fence, Ziggy glared up into the tree. That annoying squirrel had disappeared. And now that Ziggy could no longer hear or see it, he pretty much forgot all about it. Squirrel? What squirrel? It was exciting to be on the other side of the fence. That yard, and the boys on those fast machines he could chase, and that other dog—they had all been quite interesting for a while. But now he was ready for some new adventures. He looked around. Which way should he go? Hmmm...so many choices. And it was hard to concentrate with that boy yelling his name over and over. Then something caught his eye. Hey, was that a cat?

Ziggy couldn't be sure, but there was only one way to find out.

"Ziggy! Ziggy!" Ziggy ignored Charles's calls, and Charles couldn't do anything but watch through the fence as Ziggy looked this way and that. "Come, Ziggy! Please come back!" called Charles. But the puppy just sniffed the air, then took off diagonally across the neighbors' back-yard. "Oh, no," groaned Charles. "I think he spotted the Galluccis' cat."

The Galluccis' yard was a tangle of bushes and vines and fallen trees. Charles thought quickly. He knew there was no point in trying to climb over the fence. It would be impossible to catch Ziggy in that mess. "Quick," he said to his friends, "grab your bikes. We'll have to go around the block to catch him."

Charles picked up Buddy and dashed to the back door. "Ziggy ran away," he yelled. "But we'll catch him. Don't worry!" He didn't even wait to hear Mom's response. He just shoved Buddy inside and took off with a flying leap back down the stairs. He grabbed his bike. "You go that way," he told Sammy, pointing. "See if you can cut him off by the Schneiders' driveway. David and I will go the other way in case he heads toward the Dodsons'."

Charles pedaled as hard as he could. David, always a fast rider, kept right up. "Wait, what if he runs back toward your house?" David asked when they stopped at a corner to wait for a safe time to cross the road.

"Good point," Charles said. "Maybe you should go back there. Then we'd have all the directions covered."

David peeled off back toward the Petersons' house, and Charles kept going, taking a left and then another left to end up all the way around the block, near the front of the Galluccis' house. Mrs. Gallucci was out in the front yard, raking leaves.

"Hi there, Charles." She waved at him. "You sure are in a hurry today."

"Did you see a dog?" Charles put one foot down and leaned into his bike. He was breathing hard and his heart pounded. "A puppy? Did a little puppy come this way?"

"Did your Buddy run away?" Mrs. Gallucci asked. "Oh, dear."

"No, not Buddy," said Charles. "It's a puppy we're fostering. A dachshund. He's really little" — he held his hands out to show Ziggy's size — "about this big. He's black and tan. He dug under our fence and went into your backyard. Did you see him?"

Mrs. Gallucci shook her head. "I didn't," she said. "But now that I think about it, George did come tearing around the house just a couple of minutes ago, like something was chasing him."

George was the Galluccis' black-and-white cat. So Ziggy *had* spotted him. But where had Ziggy gone after chasing George? Charles could not believe this was happening. No foster puppy had ever run away before.

Sammy rode up. "Did you see him?" he asked Charles.

Charles shook his head. "Did you?"

Sammy shook his head, too. "No runaway puppy back that way," he said.

Charles sighed. This was awful. How could he have lost Ziggy already? He'd only had him for a couple of hours.

"We'll find him," said Sammy, as if he could read Charles's mind. "Come on. Let's ride around."

First they checked the Galluccis' backyard, pushing through branches and vines, but Ziggy was nowhere in sight. Then they rode back to Charles's house to check in with David, in case Ziggy had gone there. He had not. Then the three boys rode all over the neighborhood and even downtown, peering into every backyard and under every parked car. Charles began to worry.

He saw a lot of places for a little dog to hide and a lot of ways for a little dog to get hurt. "Ziggy," they called. "Ziggy, where are you?"

There was no sign of a wiener dog.

Ziggy had disappeared.

"I better go home," David said finally. "It's almost dark."

"Me, too," said Sammy.

Charles swallowed hard so he would not cry. "Okay," he said. "Thanks, you guys." David rode off toward his house, and Sammy and Charles headed back to their block.

"Don't worry," said Sammy as he got off his bike in front of his house. "Ziggy will turn up. Maybe he's even home right now."

He wasn't. But Lizzie and Dad were, and they wanted to meet the newest foster pup. "Where's Ziggy?" asked Lizzie.

Charles gulped. "I—He—" he began. And then he *did* start to cry. He told the whole story through his sobs while Mom rubbed his back and Dad knelt down in front of him, asking serious questions and nodding as Charles explained.

Lizzie didn't rub his back. Lizzie was mad. "How could you?" she asked. "How could you lose a puppy we're supposed to be taking care of? This has never happened before."

That made Charles start crying all over again, but then he saw Mom put a hand on Lizzie's shoulder. "It wasn't exactly your brother's fault," she said. "You heard Charles. Ziggy dug a hole underneath the fence."

"If I had been home, I would have warned everybody about that," said Lizzie, a little more gently. "Dachshunds are diggers. That's what they were bred for, to tunnel underground and chase off badgers and things."

Charles didn't know what a badger was, but he was sure Ziggy could catch one if they lived underground. He had never seen a dog dig like that before.

"It's nobody's fault," said Mom. "It just happened.

We can walk around the neighborhood some more after dinner, but then we're just going to have to go to bed and hope that Ziggy comes back. I don't know what else we can do tonight."

"We should call your aunt Amanda," said Dad.

Charles felt his stomach flip. "And Rosie, too," he said. "If Ziggy doesn't come back soon, we'll have to tell Rosie."

CHAPTER SIX

Ziggy was having the time of his life. He was free and on his own. He was seeing things he'd never seen before, smelling smells he'd never smelled before. What fun. After he chased the cat, he discovered the scent of another animal, something wild-smelling and exciting. He followed that trail to a garbage can that had been knocked over, and had a delicious snack of half a rotten banana and some burnt toast. Yum! A drink out of a nearby puddle topped it off, and he was ready for more action. Where to next? He trotted down the street, hardly noticing that the sun was fading, the air was growing cooler, and night was coming on....

When Ziggy did not turn up by the time it was dark, Charles called Aunt Amanda. She was upset to hear that Ziggy had escaped, but not exactly surprised. "That little dog is a real adventurer," she said. "You must feel terrible, but remember, it's not your fault. I suppose there's not much we can do to find him now. I'd say there's a good chance he'll show up by tomorrow morning when he gets hungry. Let's wait until then to call Rosie."

By bedtime Charles's voice was hoarse from calling Ziggy's name and his eyes were scratchy and tired from crying. He did not sleep very well that night. First he was too hot, and he threw off all his covers. Then he was too cold. He kept getting up to go to the bathroom. Four times Charles thought he heard a puppy whimpering, but when he ran downstairs in his bare feet and pajamas and opened the door, Ziggy was nowhere in sight. Finally, he curled up with Buddy on the rug next to his bed and fell asleep on the floor.

When he woke up in the morning, he raced downstairs to look for Ziggy. The backyard was empty, and so was the front. No Ziggy. Charles stood at the door, picturing the puppy's soft brown eyes and happy expression. Did Ziggy still look happy after a night on the streets all alone? Was he safe? Had he found a place to sleep? Something to eat? Charles's heart ached when he thought about it. *Please, please be okay, Ziggy,* he thought. It was an awfully big world out there for such a little puppy.

He ate some cornflakes — not that he had much of an appetite — and got ready for school before he finally faced the fact that he had to call Rosie. Mom offered to do it for him, but Charles knew that he should be the one to tell Rosie that Ziggy had run off. After all, he had been watching Ziggy when it had happened.

Rosie gasped when Charles called to tell her. "Gone? Already?" she asked. "Oh, dear. Oh, Ziggy." Charles thought he heard her sniff, as if she were crying. "And I can't even help. I have to leave town today to lead a training seminar." Then she began to tell Charles everything he needed to do. "You'll have to call the local animal control people, and the police, and the animal shelter. Let them know that Ziggy is lost in case someone finds him and turns him in. Make up some posters—there are examples online." She rattled off the name of a website. "Post them all over the neighborhood, and make flyers to put in people's mailboxes, and give them to the mailman and delivery people and anybody else you can think of. And—"

Charles gulped. How was he going to do all this? He had to go to school in about ten minutes. Mom took the phone from Charles. "Rosie?" she asked. "This is Betsy Peterson. Charles is leaving for school, but I'll be home today. What can I do?" She waved Charles off as she sat at the kitchen table and began to write things down.

Charles and Sammy watched for Ziggy and called his name over and over as they rode their bikes to school, but there was no sign of the puppy. Charles's cornflakes turned into a lump in his stomach. How could he have let Ziggy run off? How would he ever find him? Would anybody ever let his family foster another puppy after this?

At morning meeting Charles told the whole story, with help from Sammy and David. Somehow, Charles managed not to cry while he explained how Ziggy had run away. But his teacher, Mr. Mason, must have been able to tell how upset he was.

"Okay." Mr. Mason clapped his hands as they finished their meeting. "Here's what we're going to do. We're going to make finding Ziggy our class project."

"Really?" At first Charles didn't understand what his teacher meant. But when Mr. Mason explained, Charles got it. And as the day went on, the lump in Charles's stomach began to get smaller.

First Mr. Mason found the website Rosie had mentioned, with the sample LOST posters on it. For language arts, he had the class decide what Ziggy's poster should say. "Give me some adjectives, some words that describe Ziggy," he said to Charles. He stood at the blackboard, ready to write them down.

"Curious?" Charles said.

"Black and tan," Sammy shouted.

"Fast," David added.

"Short!" yelled a girl named Lucy. That made Charles laugh.

For math, Mr. Mason had the class figure out how many weeks it would take Charles to save up the allowance money for the reward he wanted to offer.

He had the class make a map of Charles's neighborhood, so they could begin to chart Ziggy's movements. So far, there were only two red pushpins in the map: Charles's house and the Galluccis' yard. Once the posters and flyers were printed up—with a picture they found online of a dachshund who looked just like Ziggy—Mr. Mason made dozens of copies and handed them out so everyone could color in the big LOST headline at the top. "That'll get some attention," he said.

By the end of the day, most of the kids in Charles's class had volunteered to help search their neighborhoods for Ziggy, put up posters, and hand out flyers. They had researched what to do when your dog is lost, and they were ready to put the first steps into action.

By the time Charles and Sammy biked home, Charles had completely forgotten about the lump in his stomach. It felt good to be *doing* something. At home, he showed Mom and Lizzie the posters, and Mom told him about the calls she had made to animal shelters, vets, and the police. She had also put a special message on the answering machine and her cell phone so that if anyone called to report seeing Ziggy, they would know that they had the right number.

"I'll go out on my bike and put up posters," Charles said after he'd had a quick snack. "Lizzie, you can walk Buddy around the neighborhood and call Ziggy. On the Internet it said that sometimes a runaway dog will come up to you if you're with another dog he likes."

Lizzie raised her eyebrows. "Look who's bossy now," she said. Usually *she* was the one who ordered people around. But she went and got Buddy's leash.

While Lizzie walked Buddy, Charles and Sammy and David rode all over the neighborhood. They put a flyer in every mailbox and posters on every telephone pole. They talked to all the neighbors they saw, telling them about Ziggy. And they looked everywhere for the adventurous little wiener dog—but he was nowhere to be seen.

Charles was still glad to be taking action, but by the time he, Sammy, and David ran out of flyers and posters, he had begun to feel discouraged. Nobody had seen Ziggy anywhere, and it had now been almost twenty-four hours since he had run off. But when he got home, Mom met him at the door, all excited.

"We just got a call!" she said. She was still clutching the phone. "Somebody saw Ziggy, down by Fable Farm."

CHAPTER SEVEN

Ziggy's feet hurt, and he had to keep stopping to lick them. Licking his feet made him thirsty. Being thirsty reminded him how hungry he was; the only thing he had eaten all day was a dried-up old apple core he had found on the side of the road. He had something stuck in his fur that made his whole leg itchy, and a stupid cat had scratched him on the nose when he had tried to nibble just a tiny bite of food out of her bowl on someone's back porch. He had a feeling it would get dark again soon, and he wanted to find a safe, quiet spot to sleep. He could sort of remember a place where a nice lady gave out lots of pats and good food, and where he could always find a soft bed and another dog or two to curl up with. Maybe he would find a place like that again someday. But meanwhile, he was still having fun—wasn't he?

Charles raced down the street on his bike, Mom's cell phone tucked safely into his pocket. Ziggy! Finally, someone had seen the little pup. Charles couldn't wait to gather him into his arms and give him a great big hug. He couldn't wait to tell Rosie that Ziggy was okay. She would be so relieved.

Charles did not usually ride his bike all the way to the farm stand where his parents bought vegetables in the summer. Fable Farm was outside his normal territory, in an area he had been meaning to explore more. Mom and Dad had given him permission to ride there; Mom had even ridden with him one day the past fall so they could map out the safest roads. Sammy was allowed to ride there, too. But David did not have permission yet, so the three of them had been sticking closer to home.

"I'll come pick you and Ziggy up as soon as you call me," Mom had said as she'd handed over her cell phone. "By the time you get there, your dad will be home to watch the Bean." She had not wanted to take the time to get the Bean dressed and into his car seat. Lately the Bean had been very annoyed by his shoes, and every time she dressed him it turned into a big battle, complete with tantrums and tears.

Charles pedaled down the unfamiliar streets. At first it was exciting to ride in a whole new place. He wondered why Ziggy had wandered so far. What could that puppy be looking for? There wasn't much out this way: there were no stores, no restaurants, and fewer houses.

Then, at a stop sign, Charles paused. Was he supposed to turn right or left here? Or maybe go straight? It had not seemed so confusing when he had biked here with Mom. Charles suddenly wished he had just waited with her until Dad had come home.

He looked around until he caught sight of a church steeple ahead. The farm stand was right down the road from a church. Charles began to ride again, standing up to push hard on the pedals.

He was panting by the time he rode up to the farm stand. He got off his bike and leaned it against a fence. The farm stand's bins were empty except for a few leftover corn husks and one soft, rotting pumpkin. It was almost hard to picture the way it looked in summer, when the bins overflowed with tomatoes, lettuce, and corn.

Charles walked around to the back of the stand. Where was Ziggy? Where was anybody? "Hello?" he called. A door banged open and a woman and a little blond girl appeared. Jesy and her daughter Meridian. Charles remembered them both from his summer visits to Fable Farm.

"Hi. We were just tidying up in there. Are you the one looking for a dog?" Jesy smiled at Charles while Meridian ducked behind her mom.

Charles nodded. "Ziggy. He's a dachshund. Black and tan. About this big." He held out his hands. "Did you catch him? Where is he?"

But Jesy shook her head. "I'm so sorry," she said. "I don't think it was your dog after all. The one we saw was much bigger, maybe more like the size of a basset hound." She held out *her* hands, much farther apart. "And it had big white spots."

Charles stared at her. "A basset hound?" He took a step back. Not Ziggy. Not Ziggy after all. He wasn't going to be picking Ziggy up and hugging him. He wasn't going to be calling Rosie. Ziggy was still lost.

The phone rang in Charles's pocket. "Do they have him?" Mom asked eagerly when he answered. "I can be there in five minutes."

Once again, Charles felt like crying. "No," he said.

"What?" Mom asked. "What did you say? I can hardly hear you."

"No," Charles said into the phone. "No, it wasn't him."

"Oh," said Mom. "Oh." She was quiet for a moment.

"Can you...can you come pick me up?" Charles asked. He just wanted to be home.

"Sure," said Mom. "Stay right there."

While he waited, Meridian told Charles about *her* puppy. "She's black and white and her name's Celina," she said, looking up at Charles with big blue eyes as she scrunched the hem of her skirt. "She likes to herd the ducks, and she sleeps on my bed. Once she peed on the couch."

Charles nodded and smiled, but he wasn't really listening. The phone rang again in his pocket. "Hello?" He hoped it wasn't Mom saying she would be late.

"Is this the person who's looking for a dog?" asked a man.

Charles's heart thumped. "A dachshund," he said. "A puppy. Black and tan. Did you see him?"

"He's in my front yard right now," said the man.

Mom pulled up in the van as Charles was getting directions. "Let's go," Charles said to her. "Ziggy's over on Gould Hill Road!"

Charles said good-bye to Jesy and Meridian while Mom put his bike in the van. "I hope you find your puppy," said Jesy. "Good luck," she called as they drove off.

Charles saw Ziggy the minute Mom pulled up in front of the house. The puppy was still in the yard, gobbling kibble out of a metal bowl. His coat did not look as shiny as it had the day before, and his tail was not wagging. But it was definitely Ziggy. Charles let out a big breath as he undid his seat belt. *Finally.*

"Ziggy!" Charles leapt out of the car, slamming the door behind him. He ran toward Ziggy. He could not wait to scoop that puppy up into his arms and take him home.

Ziggy raised his head, took one look at Charles, and zipped out of sight around the corner of the house.

CHAPTER EIGHT

Ziggy ran as fast as he could, scrambling around a corner and pushing through some bushes. That person's voice was familiar, but why did he have to shout and run that way? That was scary! Lots of people had shouted at Ziggy lately—for example, when he'd cut across a field where boys and girls were kicking a ball—and some of them had even tried to grab him. Who knew where they would have taken him if they'd caught him? It could have been anywhere. And anywhere was not where Ziggy wanted to be. Ziggy was tired of adventuring. More than anything, he wanted to be at that place he remembered, the place with the nice lady and the other dogs. He wasn't sure why *he'd had to leave in the first place, but now it was up to him to find his way home.*

Charles stood with his hands helplessly at his sides as he watched Ziggy zip out of sight. What was the *matter* with that little pup? Didn't he understand that Charles wanted to help him? To love him? To give him a safe, warm place to stay?

Mom came up behind Charles and put her hands on his shoulders. "Don't worry. Now at least we know he's still okay. We'll keep driving around, and I bet we'll get another call soon. Somebody's bound to see him."

Mom was right. The next call came before they'd even finished buckling their seat belts. It was Dad, reporting that someone had called their home phone. "She said Ziggy ran through her kids' sandbox a minute ago," he said, then gave Charles an address on Jacobs Road. "Also, Rosie just called. She decided to cancel her workshop so she could help find Ziggy. I told her where you're heading and she said she'll meet you there."

Charles did not look forward to facing Rosie. He felt terrible about letting Ziggy get away again. He knew how much she loved that puppy.

He and Mom got to Jacobs Road first. They drove slowly up a long hill, watching both sides of the road for Ziggy, but he was nowhere in sight. "I guess he's still on the move," Mom said. "Who knows which way he went this time?" She pulled into the driveway at the address Dad had given them, and a woman came to the door of the house, shaking her head.

"Gone," she called. She pointed up the hill. "He went that way."

Before Mom could back their van out of the driveway, another van pulled in behind them. Charles knew that it must be Rosie as soon as he saw the I ♡ MY DACHSHUND bumper sticker and the license plate that said DOXIES. Sure enough, the door opened and Rosie jumped out. "Is he here?" she asked hopefully. Then she must have seen the look on Mom's face. "I guess not," she said. She slumped against her van. "Poor little dude," she said.

"It's my fault," Charles said. He couldn't stop himself. "I let Ziggy get away in the first place, and then, when I had the chance to get him back, I just scared him off. He ran away from me so fast..." He knew it was silly to have his feelings hurt by a dog, but they were.

But Rosie shook her head. "Not your fault at all," she said. "Even I didn't know Ziggy could dig like that, or I would have warned you. And as for him running away from you, that happens all the time when people try to catch a lost dog. By the time they've been out on their own for a day or so, most dogs are pretty freaked out. Any fast movement scares them." She reached into her van and pulled out a folder. "This is my 'What to Do When Your Dog Is Lost' folder. I've been through this before, and I've found lots of good advice in books and online."

Charles hung his head. "I should have known not to run toward Ziggy," he said. "I was just so excited to see him. So how can you ever catch a dog if he runs away as soon as he sees you?" Charles asked.

"Well," Rosie said, "for one thing, it's a good idea to always have some treats in your pocket and a leash in your hand when you're looking for a runaway dog. You want to be able to coax him toward you if you see him. Let the dog come to you, and act like you don't even care. Stay very still, and just hold those treats out. Sometimes you can toss pieces of meat or cheese toward the dog, tempting him to come closer and closer."

Charles remembered doing that with Lucky, a stray dog he and David had once tried to catch. "I bet Ziggy's pretty hungry by now." Charles pictured the puppy gulping down the bowl of kibble in that man's yard.

Rosie nodded. "Exactly. Some kind of special food will look and smell extra yummy to him." She rummaged in her van again and brought out a package of hot dogs. "He will not be able to resist these, I guarantee."

"But what if we don't get another chance?" Charles asked.

"Well, there is one other way," said Rosie. She pointed to the back of her van, where Charles saw a big metal box. It looked sort of like the dog crates his family used for training puppies. "That's a humane trap," said Rosie. "'Humane' means it won't hurt a dog at all, but if he goes into it, he won't be able to get out until a person lets him out. If we get some more sightings, we can set it up in the area where we think Ziggy is roaming. We bait it with these"—she held up the hot dogs—"and wait for him to catch himself."

At that moment, Mom's phone rang. She answered it, talked for a minute, then hung up. "Another sighting." She started up the car. "Let's go."

Rosie followed them to the next address, and the next, and the next. The calls kept coming in until it began to grow dark, but every time they got to a place where Ziggy had been seen, they were disappointed to find him already gone. They had driven farther and farther away from the Petersons' house, and there was no sign anywhere of the little dachshund.

"We might as well call it a day," said Rosie finally, once the calls had slowed down. "Most dogs out on their own will find a safe place to rest once it gets dark."

They set up Rosie's humane trap in the backyard of a nice man who had called to report seeing Ziggy drink out of his birdbath. After Rosie had baited it with hot dogs, she gave Charles a hug. "Don't worry," she said. "My Ziggy is a scrappy little guy. And it's a real good sign that he's been seen so many times. We'll find him, you wait and see."

CHAPTER NINE

Ziggy was sure he was going the right way. He could just feel it in his bones. He was tired — but he had to keep moving. Every time he stopped somewhere, people shouted at him or tried to catch him. Once, he thought he heard a familiar voice call his name. He stopped in his tracks and listened, sniffing the air. Every one of his whiskers quivered as he sniffed and listened and looked around. There it was again, a faint voice, calling his name. It was the nice lady! Ziggy dashed toward the voice. He ran as fast as he could and soon he smelled her, too. She had walked on this ground only moments earlier. And then he could see her. Oh, joy! She had her back to him, but in a moment she would turn and smile at him and call his name, and he would run to her and she would pick him up and take him home to that place he remembered.

But the lady did not turn around. Instead, she climbed into her big house on wheels—Ziggy remembered riding in that—and the house moved down the road. Ziggy chased it, barking, but it did not hear him. It just ran off, much too fast for him to ever catch it.

"Don't worry," Rosie had told Charles. But how could he *stop* worrying? All he could think about was Ziggy and where he might be and whether he was scared, or hungry, and how they were ever, ever going to find him. And even though Rosie kept saying that everything would work out all right, Charles was pretty sure that she was worrying, too. How could anyone *not* worry about a little puppy out there in the big world all by himself?

At school the next day, Charles reported the

latest Ziggy news during morning meeting. All the other kids reported on what they'd been doing, too. Everybody had been putting up posters, talking to people, and handing out flyers. It made Charles feel a little better to hear that his friends were out searching for Ziggy, too.

But as the day went on, Charles couldn't concentrate on anything but Ziggy. He got six words wrong on his spelling quiz because he wasn't paying attention. He could not remember his three-times table. And he totally messed up his oral report on otters.

Nobody else seemed to be paying attention to their lessons, either. Finally, Mr. Mason pulled out the neighborhood map the class had made the day before. "Let's get back to our Find Ziggy project, shall we?" he asked.

He had Charles tell him all the places where Ziggy had been sighted, and he stuck red pushpins in all those spots. Charles sat at his desk with his chin on one hand, remembering how frustrating it had been to arrive too late every time. What good was it to replay the whole thing in his mind?

"Hmmm, that's interesting," said Mr. Mason. "It almost looks as if the pins are in a pattern."

Charles sat up and took a closer look at the map. Mr. Mason was right. The pins started on one side of the map and meandered toward the other, from right to left, east to west. West. Toward West Springfield, the town where Rosie lived, across the bridge. Charles remembered that he and Aunt Amanda had gone over that bridge the day they had picked up Ziggy. He jumped up. "I think Ziggy's trying to find his way home," he said. "He's trying to get back to Rosie's." He told Mr. Mason where Rosie lived.

Mr. Mason nodded slowly as he examined the map. "You might be right," he said. "And it would not be that surprising. There are lots of stories about lost dogs finding their way home, even over a distance of hundreds of miles. Nobody knows exactly how they manage to do it, but they do."

Charles called Rosie as soon as he got home from school. "Maybe we should set a humane trap near your house, too," he told her. "In case Ziggy comes back when you're not around."

"That's an excellent idea," said Rosie.

Charles thought she sounded tired. "Any more Ziggy sightings today?" he asked.

"I almost hate to tell you," said Rosie. "Somebody called me to say that Ziggy had been caught in that trap we set for him. I zoomed over there as fast as I could, but by the time I got there, another person had come along and let him out."

"What?" Charles couldn't believe his ears. "Why would they do that?"

Rosie gave a short laugh. "I think they felt sorry for the poor dog and wanted to set him free," she said. "Next time I'll remember to attach one of our flyers to the humane trap so people understand what it's there for."

It made Charles feel a little better to know that Rosie made mistakes, too. He was just about to tell her not to worry, they would try again and catch Ziggy for real the next time, when Mom came over, waving her cell phone.

"Hold on," Charles told Rosie. "What is it?" he asked Mom.

"Somebody caught Ziggy," she said. "It's him, I'm sure. They gave me a perfect description. They're driving over with him now."

Charles grinned at her. Mom seemed just as excited as he was. "That's great," he said. He spoke into the phone again. "Rosie? Did you hear that?" he asked.

"I'm on my way," Rosie said, and hung up.

A few minutes later, a little blue car pulled up in front of the Petersons' house. Charles looked out the window in the front door. Were these the people with Ziggy? He decided to wait until he saw that Ziggy was safely clipped to a leash before he ran out to meet them. He had learned his lesson. He did not want to scare Ziggy off.

Charles watched and waited. Yes! There, in the backseat, was a small black and tan puppy, poking his sharp little nose up to look out the window. It was Ziggy, all right. Charles would have recognized those eyes anywhere. It looked as if he had a collar on, with a red leash clipped to it. Then, just as a woman got out of the passenger side of the car and opened its back door, Lizzie came downstairs from her room and joined Charles at the window.

"What's going on?" she asked. Then she must have spied the little dog. "Hey, is that Ziggy?"

Before Charles could stop her, she opened the door and ran out, slamming it behind her. "Ziggy!" she shouted.

And Ziggy took off, dragging his red leash behind him.

CHAPTER TEN

Ziggy couldn't believe it. After all the time he had put into trying to find his way home, there he was, back where he had started when he first dug under the fence. Not that it was a bad place. In fact, it was pretty good compared to sleeping under a bush and eating garbage. He had liked the other puppy who lived at this place, and the boy and the little person were kind. Still, it wasn't home. By this time, Ziggy really, really wanted to be home. But with this leash attached, what could he do? He got out of the car and began to walk toward the house. That was when the door slammed and a person yelled his name and galloped toward him. Not again. Ziggy was tired of being chased. But

his fear overcame his exhaustion, and once again,
Ziggy ran.

"Oops," said Lizzie. She put her hand over her mouth and stared down the street toward where Ziggy had run. "That was dumb. I can't believe I did that, especially after hearing what happened when *you* did it."

Charles had followed Lizzie outside. He glared at her. Then he sighed and shook his head. "I know how it is," he said. "I got excited when I saw him the first time, too. Don't worry. I'll find him, and I'll catch him. I know what to do." He ran to the kitchen, grabbed two hot dogs out of the fridge, put them into a plastic bag, and shoved the bag into his pocket. He buckled on his helmet and headed for the garage to get his bike.

Lizzie must have told Mom what happened, because before Charles could leave Mom ran out after him. "Here, take this." She handed him her cell phone. "We'll stay here in case somebody calls in a sighting on the other phone."

Charles did not stop to wonder which way to go. First of all, he had seen Ziggy run up the street toward the Schneiders' house. Second, he knew from looking at the pins on the map at school that Ziggy was most likely heading west again, trying to find his way back to Rosie's. Charles pedaled as hard as he could until his legs burned and he could hardly catch his breath. He checked every yard as he rode past the familiar houses of his neighborhood. He strained his eyes for even a glimpse of black and tan, but he did not see Ziggy anywhere.

"How far could he get in such a short time?" Charles said to himself as he coasted down the hill past the Hartmullers' low one-story house, surrounded by apple and plum trees and rose-bushes. Mom said Uncle Henry, as everyone called him, had a real green thumb.

"Ziggy, where are you?" Charles sang out as he ground on the pedals, making his way slowly back up the hill, past the DeZagos', where the swimming pool lay covered for the winter. He peered into the Crables' garage and up the stone stairs that wound through a blanket of ivy to the Dodsons' house.

Ziggy was nowhere in sight.

Then Charles rode over the top of the hill, where the Conklins' house sat, with its view of the woods and the stream. If Ziggy had gone into the woods, it might take forever to find him. Charles remembered when he and David had tried to catch Lucky, that stray dog who had been living in the woods behind David's house. It had taken days.

But then...there he was. Ziggy stood in the doorway of the Conklins' barn, sniffing at the dark inside, where thirteen chickens lived. They laid the eggs Charles often ate for breakfast. Ziggy's back was to Charles, and his rear legs quivered with curiosity as he stared inside the barn. Charles thought Ziggy had probably never smelled chickens before.

Slowly, quietly, Charles got off his bike and laid it on the ground. He stuck a hand into his pocket and pulled out a hot dog. He took a few silent steps closer to Ziggy, then sat down on the ground. He knew just what to do now. He broke off a piece of hot dog and tossed it gently in Ziggy's direction.

Ziggy must have heard the soft noise of the hot dog piece plopping into the dirt behind him. He turned around quickly. Charles stayed very, very still. Aunt Amanda had once told him that dogs did not see nearly as well as they smelled, and that mostly what caught their attention was movement.

Sure enough, Ziggy did not seem startled, even when his eyes met Charles's. Maybe he was so hungry that the smell of hot dog was all he could think about. He sniffed and sniffed again. Then he took a few quick steps forward, dragging his red leash behind him, and snatched the hot dog piece. He gobbled it up.

Slowly, slowly, Charles raised his hand and tossed another piece so that it landed a little closer to his own knee. Ziggy took a few more steps and grabbed the food. "Good boy," Charles whispered softly. He threw another piece, and another, and Ziggy found them and chomped them. In another minute, Ziggy was almost close enough to touch. But Charles waited patiently. The last thing he wanted to do was scare Ziggy off now.

Slowly, Charles pulled the other hot dog out of his pocket. He held his breath as he put it on the ground right in front of him. A whole hot dog. That would take Ziggy more than a second to eat.

Ziggy inched his way over to the hot dog, keeping an eye on Charles. Then he took one step closer and caught up the hot dog in his mouth.

Quick as a flash, Charles reached out and grabbed Ziggy's collar. In another second, he held the red leash in his hands. "Gotcha," he said very quietly.

Ziggy finished eating the hot dog and looked up at Charles. Then he rolled over onto his back and waved his paws in the air.

I surrender! You caught me. Can I go home now?

Charles heard a car drive up behind him. He stood, holding Ziggy's leash, and turned around to see Rosie's van pulling into the Conklins' drive-way. He could see her face through the windshield. Rosie was crying.

She stepped out of the van and came over to kneel in front of Ziggy. "You found him," she said to Charles. "You found my boy." She scooped Ziggy into her arms and kissed him. She hugged him. She nuzzled his face with her chin. And the whole time, tears streamed down her cheeks. "I will never let you out of my sight again," Charles heard her say to Ziggy.

"You mean—?" Charles began.

Rosie nodded. "I'm keeping this boy. I missed him so much when he was gone that I knew I could never let someone else have him. My husband will just have to get used to eleven dachshunds. Maybe we'll put an addition on the house."

Charles smiled and reached out to pat Ziggy's head. He knew that Rosie's place was the perfect home for the pup. "I know he'll be happy to be home with you," he said. "That's all he wanted, the whole time he was out there. He just wanted to be home."

PUPPY TIPS

What should you do if *you* lose your pet? It can be scary and sad if your pet runs away or gets lost. But taking action, the way Charles did, can make you feel better — and can help find your pet! There is a lot of information on the Internet about finding lost pets. But the most important things are:

1) Spread the information. Tell everyone from the police to workers at the park that your dog is lost. Make flyers and posters that tell people what your pet looks like and where to call if he's seen.

2) Keep looking! It's easy to get discouraged if you don't find your pet right away. But stick with it, and with luck your pet will be found.

Dear Reader,

When I was a little girl, my very first pet was a beautiful tortoiseshell kitten named Jenny. When she didn't come home for two days, I was very upset. I put up signs all over the neighborhood. I still have one! It says:

LOST: A tortoiseshell kitten named Jenny with a small white stripe on the side of her neck. With four black and one white paws. If found, I will be greatly relieved and happy. 20¢ reward. Thank you. Sincerely, Ellen Miles.

I was lucky: Jenny did come home and we had many happy years together after that.

Yours from the Puppy Place,
Ellen Miles

P.S. To read about another energetic little pup, check out RASCAL.

THE PUPPY PLACE

DON'T MISS THE NEXT PUPPY PLACE ADVENTURE!

Here's a peek at BELLA!

Lizzie knelt down to take a closer look at the puppy in the shoebox. Ms. Dobbins had set up a lamp over her box to keep her warm. In its golden glow, the puppy stretched and squirmed in her sleep. She opened her tiny mouth and yawned a pink puppy yawn. She was so young she didn't even have teeth yet! Lizzie felt her heart flip over. The puppy was only a few inches long, and mostly white with orangey-red spots like freckles. One ear was the same orangey-red color and the other was white. Her nose was pink, and her tiny paws were, too. Her ears were just little flaps, about the size of Lizzie's pinkie fingernail.

Now the puppy opened her mouth and made a little mewing noise, almost like a kitten. "Oh!" said Lizzie. The puppy looked up at her with milky blue eyes that did not quite seem to focus on her face. "Wow, her eyes are barely open." She wanted to reach out a finger and stroke the puppy, but she was afraid she might hurt her. "How old is she?"

"Just about four weeks," said Ms. Dobbins. "She's on her own and will need to be fed from a bottle."

Lizzie looked down at the puppy. She didn't look much like the cocker spaniels on her "Dog Breeds of the World" poster, with their long, fringed ears and adorable faces. She looked more like a hamster. A sick hamster. "The poor little thing!"

"I know," said Ms. Dobbins. "When my friend called to ask for help, I agreed to take her. How could I say no? She drove the puppy up, and showed me how to mix the formula to feed her with." She showed Lizzie a baby bottle full of white liquid. "It's made with goat's milk and raw eggs," she said. "And some other stuff. Puppies this age have to eat every three or four hours. Maybe even more often in this case, since she is not growing as fast as she should be."

"She does seem really small," said Lizzie. She gazed down at the puppy, feeling a strange mixture of love and fear. This small, squirmy thing was so helpless!

ABOUT THE AUTHOR

Ellen Miles likes to write about the different personalities of dogs. She is the author of more than 30 books, including the Puppy Place and Taylor-Made Tales series as well as *The Pied Piper* and other Scholastic Classics. Ellen loves to be outdoors every day, walking, biking, skiing, or swimming, depending on the season. She also loves to read, cook, explore her beautiful state, and hang out with friends and family. She lives in Vermont.

If you love animals, be sure to read all the adorable stories in the Puppy Place series!

SOPHIE

Sophie knows she's special — now she just needs the perfect name to show it!

SOPHIE the AWESOME
by Lara Bergen
SCHOLASTIC

SOPHIE the HERO
by Lara Bergen
SCHOLASTIC

SOPHIE the CHATTERBOX
by Lara Bergen
SCHOLASTIC

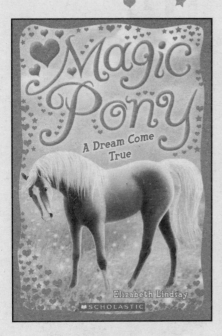